Tamara and the Sea Witch

KRYSTYNA TURSKA

PARENTS' MAGAZINE PRESS

First published in Great Britain 1971
by Hamish Hamilton Children's Books Ltd.

Copyright © 1971 by Krystyna Turska
First published in the United States of America
by Parents' Magazine Press 1972
Printed in Great Britain
ISBN: Trade 0-8193-0530-8, Library 0-8193-0531-6
Library of Congress Catalog Card Number: 70-164896

In the land of old Russia there was once a young and beautiful maiden named Tamara. She lived with her mother in a simple hut at the edge of a dark forest. The mother was too old and frail to work, and so each day Tamara went into the forest to gather mushrooms which she sold in the nearby village. In such a way she earned enough money to buy food, but it was a poor living, and there came a time when Tamara could scarcely find enough mushrooms to cover the bottom of her basket.

"Have a care, Tamara," the villagers warned her. "Do not go too far into the forest, for in the middle there is an enchanted well, round which grow the largest mushrooms ever seen. Be sure you are not tempted to pick them, for you will surely be sorry if you do."

But Tamara could not find any mushrooms at the edge of the forest, and every day she wandered further along its dark paths. So it was that one day she stumbled into a clearing, where the grass was even and green, and was sprinkled with beautiful flowers. In the middle of the clearing was a well, surrounded by the largest mushrooms she had ever seen. Strangest of all, from the well came a low sobbing sound.

Tamara knew at once that this was the enchanted well the villagers had warned her about. She turned to run away in fright, but she could not bear to return empty-handed to her mother.

As she bent swiftly to pick a few mushrooms, a voice full of sweetness came from the well: "Will you be my wife?"

Tamara did not move, so great was her fear, and a second time the voice asked, "Will you be my wife?" The voice was sad and gentle. Touched by its tenderness, Tamara turned and came nearer to the well. A third time the question was asked, "Will you be my wife?"

By now Tamara's heart was so moved by the sadness of the voice that she answered quietly, "Yes."

"Then return to your mother and worry no more," came the reply.

Tamara ran back through the forest, and when she reached the edge she stood in wonder at the sight that met her eyes. Where once had stood her humble cottage there now rose a magnificent golden palace. By the palace gates Tamara's mother waited, no longer bent and frail but radiant with happiness. As Tamara went through the gates her old rags fell from her, and she was suddenly dressed in a richly embroidered gown. Her head scarf became a diamond tiara, and on her feet appeared shoes studded with jewels.

At that moment the sun set, and a coach drawn by six black horses came through the gates. The door opened and out stepped a handsome young man. Bowing low before Tamara, he said, "I am a Prince, and by agreeing to marry me you have freed me from the enchantment of the well. You will be my bride. This palace and all its riches will be yours, and your every wish will be granted. But there is one condition," he added, "you will see me for only three days each year and I cannot tell you my name. I pray that you never ask me for it."

Soon after the wedding the Prince disappeared. Tamara was lonely and wandered sadly around the palace, wishing her husband would return. She went again to the forest and made friends with the squirrels, who became her constant companions.

One day an old woman came to the palace gate begging for food and shelter. After she had eaten, she asked to see the Princess Tamara and was taken to her.

"You have been kind to me," said the old woman, "and I wish to repay you. Tell me why you look so sad?"

So Tamara told the old woman that she loved her husband and yet could only see him for three days each year and did not even know his name. "Make the Prince tell you his name and he will stay with you for ever," said the old woman, and then she left the palace.

Tamara wept bitterly, for she knew that by her foolishness she had lost her husband. In despair she returned home, only to find the palace had vanished, and in its place she saw again the old cottage. There, too, was her mother, dressed once more in rags.

Full of grief Tamara lay down beneath a tree and slept, not knowing what to do. As she slept, an owl came to her and whispered, "Far over the sea is the island of the Sea Witch. You must go there if you wish to free your husband. But remember, never look back or your journey will be in vain. Your friends of the forest will help you." With that, the owl flew off and Tamara awoke.

"I will go at once to the island of the Sea Witch," she said. As she spoke a cormorant flew down and carried her on his back to the seashore, where she found a boat waiting, and set sail for the island.

The journey was a fearful one. The sea grew black, and the waves rose higher as hideous creatures sprang up and called to her by name. But Tamara never once looked back, and after seven days she reached a rocky island, crowned by a great dark castle, its towers and turrets rising into swirling mist.

Tamara's heart was cold with fear but she stepped boldly on to the shore, and was taken by two Guards to the court of the Sea Witch.

The Sea Witch sat upon a throne made of seashells and
coral. She was dressed in a shining green robe of seaweed,
and round her neck was coiled a venomous serpent.

In a trembling voice Tamara begged the Witch to free her husband. "Yes, my dear," said the Witch, "but first you must make me the most beautiful crown in the world from the contents of this bag. You have seven days for this task, and if you fail, you will die."

Tamara took the bag, which she found contained nothing but grains of corn. She was led to a dark tower and locked in a tiny room, with only a high barred window to let in the light.

Alone in the room Tamara wept. Suddenly she heard a chattering at the window. Looking up, she saw her friends the squirrels, and she remembered the words of the owl.

The squirrels pushed in through the bars of the window all manner of precious jewels and golden rods from which Tamara fashioned the most beautiful crown in the world. When the crown was almost finished the squirrels brought her a golden egg to put at the very top of the crown.

At the end of seven days, Tamara was brought once more to the Sea Witch.

"So," said the wicked Witch when she saw the crown, "come nearer to me and place the crown upon my head."

As Tamara approached the Witch the serpent uncoiled from her neck and drew up to spit death at the girl. But before the serpent could strike, the egg on top of the crown burst open with a crash as of thunder. Out sprang a hawk which swooped upon the serpent and destroyed it.

The Sea Witch gave a fearful shriek and in the same instant was transformed into the old woman who had come to the palace so long ago. The throne vanished in a cloud of fire and from the smoke Prince Igor emerged to claim his Princess.

The old woman, having lost her magical powers, was banished from the realm for ever. Tamara and the Prince sailed back across the sea and returned to the edge of the forest. There once more stood the palace, its towers golden in the sunlight, and waiting for them at the gates was Tamara's mother.

Freed forever from the spell of the Sea Witch, Prince Igor and the Princess Tamara lived in peace and contentment for the rest of their days.